From Your Diary with Love

Step Back In Time

On her tenth birthday,
shy Evie Denham's life
is turned around by a
special present. In the
pages of a beautiful
purple diary lies the
key to her happiness . . .

When her family moves from London to the little town of Crossacre, talented dancer Evie finds it difficult to settle in to her new life. On Evie's birthday, her mysterious neighbour, Mrs Volkov, gives her a beautiful purple velvet diary as a present. But this is no ordinary journal: every time Evie pens an entry and tucks it under her pillow overnight, she discovers the book has written back the following morning with words of guidance. Evie's diary soon becomes her treasured friend, holding the secret to her finding her feet in Crossacre, and giving her the confidence to do what she does best:

dance!

This diary is for you alone,
A secret you must keep,
Each night, tell me your worries,
And then fall sound asleep.

And as the dawn sun wakes you up,
The answer will be here,
Some words to help and guide you,
So you need have no fear.

Evie, please keep me safe and hidden,
For if anyone finds out,
These words will fade, and I'll be gone.
Of this there is no doubt.

And later, when my work is done,
Please don't put me aside.
Pass me on, wish me goodbye,
And someone else I'll guide.

Special thanks to:
Nick Baker, West Jesmond Primary School, Maney Hill
Primary School and Courthouse Junior School

EGMONT
We bring stories to life

Step Back In Time first published in Great Britain 2008
by Egmont UK Limited
239 Kensington High Street, London W8 6SA

Text & illustration © 2008 Egmont UK Ltd
Text by Nick Baker
Illustrations by Mélanie Florain

ISBN 978 1 4052 3951 6

1 3 5 7 9 10 8 6 4 2

A CIP catalogue record for this title is available
from the British Library

Typeset by Avon DataSet Ltd, Bidford on Avon, Warwickshire
Printed and bound in Great Britain by the CPI Group

From Your Diary with Love

Step Back In Time

Laura Baker

Illustrated by Mélanie Florain

EGMONT

The Denham Family

Charlie Denham

He's Evie's cool older brother who has lots of friends at school and loves playing sport, but always finds time to look out for his little sister

Evie Denham

Evie is a shy, quiet girl but with a little help and advice she hopes to make all her dancing dreams come true

Evie's Mum

She's a nurse at the local hospital and is keen for her children to feel at home in Crossacre

Evie's Dad

He's happy to have escaped city life, and when he's not enjoying the quiet surroundings of Crossacre he's running his own Internet business

Josh Denham

He's Evie's little brother. He can be a nosy pest a lot of the time, but he loves Evie really and looks up to her a lot

The Malkova Dance Academy
Students and Staff

Meera Stevens
Evie's friend and a talented artist

Lottie Dean
Thinks she's the star of The Malkova Dance Academy

Mrs Violet Swann
She's the wise principal of the dance academy who her pupils look up to

Jess Whittington
Evie's friend and a hard worker

Dame Malkova

The legendary prima ballerina who founded the academy and who still manages to inspire the students years later

Lauren Davies

Evie's friend and a natural athlete

Miss Connie Swann

She's a beautiful and kind dance teacher who always inspires her students

Matt Shanklin

He's the only boy at the academy and a reluctant dancer

Beth Dickinson

She's Evie's best friend and excellent at modern dance

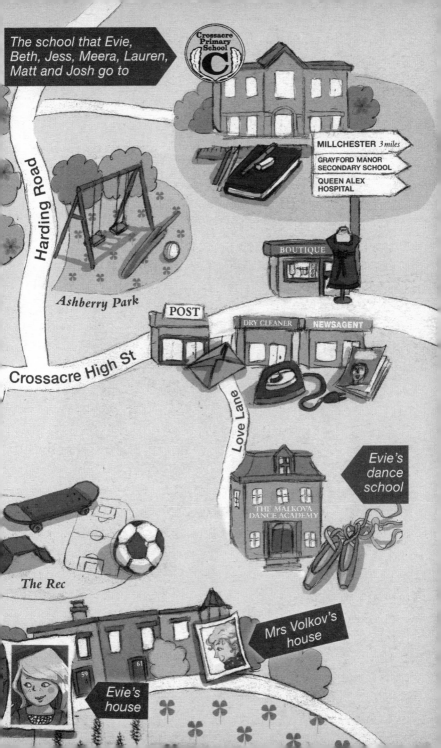

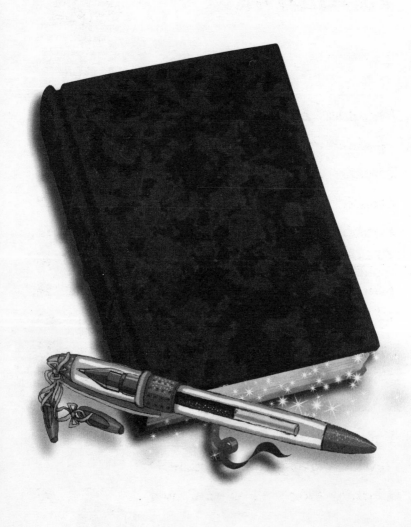

Contents

Chapter One

Sleepover Secrets

'Pass the popcorn, Evie,' said Hannah, Evie's oldest friend, as the pair snuggled up under a cosy quilt to watch *Ballet Stars* on DVD for the millionth time.

'Watch it!' squealed Hannah, as a piece of popcorn bounced off her head and wedged itself down the side of the sofa. Evie burst into giggles at her friend's horrified face.

'Right, you asked for it!' said Hannah,
launching a shower of popcorn on to Evie's head.

Soon, the pair were in fits of laughter, their legs
tangled up in the quilt as they wriggled about on
the sofa.

Red-cheeked, Evie beamed from ear to ear.
She was beginning to like her new home in
Crossacre, but there was something special about
having Hannah to stay. They had stuck together

since they first met aged three, a pair of chubby-cheeked tots who held hands and skipped together in their first ballet class. Seven years later, they still shared everything: clothes, gossip, secrets and, of course, their passion for dance.

'We'd better clean this up,' said Evie, gathering the bits of popcorn from the sofa.

'Ooh, I love this bit,' sighed Hannah, as Darcey Bussell pirouetted across the screen in a snow-white tutu. The pair had watched this part of *Swan Lake* so many times that they knew the routine off by heart.

'I wish I could dance *en pointe* like that,' said Evie, her voice full of admiration. 'Mrs Swann said I might be able to give it a go in a couple of years.'

'Brilliant!' said Hannah, hugging Evie and humming along to the famous ballet music softly.

'Oi, oi, oi!' boomed a loud voice as the bright

sitting room light glared on. It was Evie's big brother Charlie, swiftly followed by her dad and little brother Josh, who grabbed the remote control from the coffee table. The beautiful ballerina suddenly disappeared from the screen, and was replaced by a roaring football crowd.

'Football?!' the girls cried together, pulling disgusted faces.

'I'm sorry, girls,' said Mr Denham with a shrug. 'But it's the big match and we just have to watch it, I'm afraid. Millchester United don't get through to the second round of the FA Cup every day, you know!'

'Yeah, we *have* to watch it,' added Josh, handing the newly ejected DVD to Evie with a smug grin.

'There's no point in arguing,' Evie explained to Hannah. 'We'll never win when there's football involved. Come on, let's go upstairs. At least there aren't any boys up there.'

The girls stomped up to Evie's bedroom in their fluffy slippers and pyjamas, stopping to poke their tongues out at Josh and Charlie from halfway up the stairs.

Evie and Hannah jumped into the huge makeshift bed they had made on the floor earlier that day. They had piled Evie's polka-dot duvet and pillows on to a spare mattress, then added every blanket and cushion that they could find to make a cosy nest that was big enough for both of them to sleep in. The two friends soon settled down into their old sleepover routine of swapping gossip.

'Did I tell you about Mr Humphries and the frog?' Hannah whispered to Evie.

'Oh, please tell me!' said Evie, keen to catch up on the news from her old school.

'We were in the middle of assembly when suddenly Mr Humphries let out a huge yelp,' said

Hannah, her eyes sparkling in the half-light. 'He started to leap around the hall with a frog on his head! It must have jumped in through the window. I wish you'd been there, Evie.' The girls rolled around with laughter. 'Now, whenever Mr Humphries walks past, Jamie Maxwell croaks!'

Evie loved hearing stories from her old school back in London, but when she realised that she couldn't even picture Jamie Maxwell's face, she felt a little sad. *I guess I am drifting away from my old life*, she thought. *But at least I'll always have Hannah as my friend.*

The girls stayed up talking for hours, comparing stories from their dance lessons and tales of annoying little brothers. As Evie rearranged the pillows under her head, she felt something solid shift between them. Feeling around the layers of bedding, her hand began to tingle. *My diary!* she realised, running her fingers over its soft, velvet cover. *I can't believe I forgot to tell Hannah!*

Whenever Evie had a problem, her diary came up with the perfect advice. All she had to do was write about it and wait for her diary to pen a reply. Then Evie remembered her diary's request that she keep it a secret.

Please, Evie, keep me hidden,
For if anyone finds out,
These words will fade, and I'll be gone.
Of this there is no doubt.

But Evie couldn't keep the excitement to herself. She could just imagine how thrilled Hannah would be about it all. Surely it was impossible to keep a secret like that from her very best friend?

Just as Evie opened her mouth to reveal all,

Hannah sighed contentedly and rolled over to face the wall.

Realising that Hannah was asleep, Evie took a deep breath. That had been close.

Chapter Two

The Project

On Monday morning, Beth and Evie were standing in the playground wishing the bell would go so they could get inside. Joseph charged by, waving a stripy scarf and cheering loudly.

'How silly!' said Evie, laughing. 'He's even dyed his hair green and white!'

'Millchester, Millchester!' sang Lauren, racing

up to them and dancing from one foot to the other.

'Oh, not you as well!' grinned Beth.

'And what is *that*?' asked Evie, pointing at something like a glittery cabbage on Lauren's head.

'It's a Millchester United hairgrip. I made it last night. Isn't it brilliant?'

'Umm . . . yes, really . . . unusual!' smiled Evie, catching the twinkle in Beth's eye.

'You two don't seem very excited,' said Lauren.

'Well, it's only football,' said Beth.

'Only football! It's the biggest game ever! They're through to the third round of the Cup!'

After assembly, Evie sat staring gloomily from the window as Mr Mitchin handed out the history books.

Though the whole school was buzzing with excitement about next week's match, she couldn't get in the mood – after her fabulous weekend with Hannah everything now seemed dull and sad.

Giggling and gossiping together just like they used to, Evie had felt closer to her best friend than ever before, but Hannah's visit hadn't lasted nearly long enough. On Sunday afternoon, after they'd hugged goodbye, Hannah had disappeared up the road. She'd waved from the back of her mum's car and Evie had felt so lonely she'd run sobbing to her room.

Lying in bed that night, exhausted but unable to sleep, she switched on her bedside lamp, longing to share her worries with her special friend. She slid her hand under her pillow and reached for the soft velvet cover of her wonderful diary.

Dear diary,

I loved Hannah coming to stay, but now she's gone I feel so unhappy. I really wanted to go home with her, but I couldn't because I love Mum and Dad and Charlie and Josh too much. Why do nice things have to end? I wish everything could go back to how it used to be, then I wouldn't keep feeling homesick.

Evie slipped her diary back under her pillow and, comforted to have shared her thoughts, drifted at last into a gentle sleep.

Next morning, the moment she opened her eyes, Evie checked her diary.

Dear Evie,

Your weekend with Hannah sounded truly special. It is not surprising you were reminded of the fun times you used to have in London, and felt homesick.

It is always hard to leave something you love, but new friendships and adventures will always be waiting for you.

Evie paused, thinking that new adventures sounded more scary than exciting, then read on.

Sometimes, Evie, you have to be patient, but please don't worry. I'm sure things will soon settle down. Imagine you had only ever eaten plain biscuits — would you be scared to try a chocolate one, or think it an exciting treat?

Evie had stared at the page, shaking her head and wondering what biscuits had to do with anything.

'Right!' said Mr Mitchin. 'Who would like to tell me what the Ancient Romans used to eat?'

'Was it food, sir?' said Anthony with a grin.

'You are a genius!' said Mr Mitchin. 'Can anyone give me a sensible answer?'

Evie hadn't been listening. It was nearly break time and she had been puzzling about her diary's answer that morning.

'Chocolate biscuits!' she shouted, suddenly understanding what her diary meant – familiar

things, like your old school, might be very nice; but you'd never know how good a new thing could be, like a new kind of biscuit or making new friends, unless you gave it a try!

'Nice idea, Evie,' said Mr Mitchin above the laughter. 'Sadly for the Romans, it would be two thousand years before they could discover that pleasure! And talking of discoveries reminds me: you must all choose a topic to investigate for your history projects. The theme this term is the history of a local building or organisation.'

Joseph's hand shot up. 'Please, sir, can Ant and I do Millchester football club?'

'If you *promise* to wash that dye out of your hair by tomorrow!'

Mr Mitchin paused as everyone laughed, then continued. 'And I don't want you just copying facts out of books, I want you to get the *real* story.'

Talking excitedly, the class broke into groups. Jess, Meera and Lauren huddled together and quickly decided to investigate the history of Jessica's 250-year-old Georgian family house.

Beth and Evie looked at each other and smiled. They didn't need to discuss it. They knew *exactly* what to choose – The Malkova Dance Academy!

Chapter Three

New Discoveries

'Well done, everyone!' said Miss Connie at the end of Saturday morning ballet class. 'We'll warm down, then you can all get changed.'

As everyone else skipped to the changing room, Beth and Evie stood near Miss Connie, who was chatting to Mr Jacobs, the pianist.

'Please, Miss Connie,' said Evie, as Mr Jacobs put away his music, 'may we ask you something?'

'Of course, girls. What can I do for you?'

When they had finished explaining their plan to research the history of the academy, Miss Connie gave a big smile.

'What a *lovely* idea! Could you spare a few minutes now?'

Evie and Beth nodded eagerly.

As they walked along the corridor, Lottie Dean, scowling ferociously, crept out of the changing room and watched them.

'This way,' said Miss Connie, leading Evie and Beth up a creaking, spiral staircase. As they climbed, they stared at the faded photos that lined the walls.

Miss Connie noticed their interest. 'Those were all pupils from the academy,' she said. 'Some of them became quite famous.'

Perhaps one day my photo will hang up there too, thought Evie, though she felt far too shy to say so, even to Beth.

'Here we are!' said Miss Connie, opening a door. 'This is the principal's office. You may come in here *only* when invited by me or Mrs Swann.'

Evie's eyes widened. Dark oak panels lined the walls all the way up to the high ceiling. A thick red carpet covered the floor, and in the corner sat an ancient wooden desk. The room felt warm and reassuring, and Evie thought it would be a perfect place to snuggle down and listen to a story.

'Just sit there,' said Miss Connie kindly, pointing to two old brown armchairs near the fire.

As Evie and Beth sat down, Miss Connie opened a little cupboard and took out a scrumptious-looking sultana cake.

'I bring one of these every Saturday,' she said with a little smile, 'just in case we have visitors!'

Eating their cake and trying to catch all the crumbs, Evie and Beth felt very important.

'See that painting above the fire?' said Miss Connie. 'That's Anya Malkova, the lady who founded the academy.'

'Wow!' gasped Evie. 'She looks like a beautiful china doll!'

'And do you know why?' asked Miss Connie. Evie and Beth shook their heads.

'It's because she's performing *Coppélia*,' said Miss Connie. 'The ballet tells the story of a young couple, Franz and Swanilda, who are in love and about to get married. But one day, Franz sees a beautiful girl sitting on a balcony reading a book, and falls in love with her instead!'

'Oh, no!' whispered Evie.

'That's just what Swanilda thinks!' said Miss

Connie. 'So she runs away in tears. Later, Dr Coppélius, the man who owns the house, goes out. Swanilda creeps into his workshop and discovers the girl is really a life-size, clockwork doll! Suddenly, Dr Coppélius returns! Swanilda has to hide quickly, so she dresses in the doll's clothes. Then Franz comes into the shop and tells the doll that he loves her! After more misunderstandings, Franz realises the doll is Swanilda and that he loves only her, so they do marry after all.'

'Ahhh,' said Evie and Beth together.

'Well,' said Miss Connie, looking up at the picture, 'that portrait of Dame Malkova is from many years ago, when she was prima ballerina with the Bolshoi Ballet!'

'And she came to Crossacre?' said Beth, astonished to hear that anyone famous had ever visited their little town.

'Oh, yes. She –'

'Miss Connie,' interrupted Evie. 'May I borrow a pen and paper? I'd like to write this down for our project.'

As Miss Connie searched the desk for a notepad, the door behind them creaked. Beth was busy munching her cake and didn't notice, but Evie looked round. The door had opened a crack, but no one came in. *Oh*, she thought, *it's probably a gust of wind from the front door.*

'Now where was I?' said Miss Connie, passing the notepad to Evie. 'Ah, yes, Dame Malkova. She lived for ballet, and was only truly happy when dancing. For a while, she was the most famous ballerina in the world. During a tour of England, she met Marcus Brentworth, a well-known orchestral conductor. They fell deeply in love and soon married, right here in the church in Crossacre. Then, at the height of her fame, she left the Bolshoi!'

'Why?' blurted Beth, who couldn't imagine anything better than being a famous ballerina.

'Well, fame can bring many troubles. Everywhere that Dame Malkova went, crowds followed her and newspaper reporters pestered her for interviews. Rushing from one performance to another, she felt as though her life was not her own.'

The door creaked again. Evie looked up, and thought she saw a movement. Was that Lottie's furious face peering through the crack? *No*, she thought, shaking her head. *I must have imagined it.*

'After that,' Miss Connie continued, 'she decided to retire completely. However, she still loved dancing. More than anything, she wanted to pass on her love of dance as a gift to others, so she set up The Malkova Dance Academy!'

'That's amazing!' said Beth.

'Well, girls. I'm sorry, but I have to hurry off. Do please ask again if you need any more help.'

'Thank you,' whispered Evie. Then, as she shut the notepad, she heard something scurry down the stairs . . .

Chapter Four

Secret History

'Evie,' said Mum after lunch. 'Have you got ants in your pants? Go and find something to do before you drive me crazy!'

Since ballet class, Evie had been skittering around like a restless puppy, trying to understand all that Miss Connie had said. How could anyone who loved dance as much as Dame Malkova give it up? And how could being a famous prima ballerina not be the most brilliant thing in the universe?

When the phone rang she thought it might be Hannah, so she raced Josh down the hall screaming, 'I'll get it!' They both grabbed the receiver and had a tug-of-war. Evie won.

'Hello!' she said breathlessly as Josh walked sulkily back to the sitting room.

'Evie! It's Beth.'

'Wasn't that great this morning!' said Evie.

'Yes, and guess what! Mum's taking me see parish records at the church. She said we might find Dame Malkova's marriage certificate, and could even discover where she lived.'

'That's brilliant!' said Evie, hoping Beth would invite her along too.

'Sorry,' said Beth, 'but I've got to go. Mum's waiting in the car. I'll write everything down and bring it to school on Monday. Bye!'

'Bye,' Evie said, wishing there were something *she* could do for their project. Then she had a brainwave. *I'll have my own secret project – I'll discover the history of my diary!*

Mum was working a late shift at the hospital so Dad had cooked his speciality dinner – baked beans on toast.

Charlie and Evie were at the table, waiting as Josh washed his hands at the kitchen sink.

'Hurry up, Josh,' Dad said. 'Dinner's getting cold.'

'Last one to the table misses next week's match!' teased Charlie.

'No!' wailed Josh. 'That's not fair!'

'Don't worry, son,' said Dad with a smile. 'We can all watch it. Even Evie, if she wants to.'

'I'd rather do my homework, thanks,' said Evie seriously.

'Josh,' announced Charlie. 'You've got a weird sister!'

'So have you!' said Josh, and they all laughed.

'Actually,' Evie said firmly, 'I'm quite normal. It's people who watch football that are weird. I'm interested in important things, like history. I bet you didn't know that Ancient Romans never had chocolate biscuits.'

'I want chocolate biscuits!' said Josh, who hadn't even finished his beans. Dad rolled his eyes.

'How do you tell the age of a book, Dad?' said Evie.

'That's easy. Just look inside the cover. The date will be printed on the first page.'

'No, I mean *really* old books,' said Evie.

'Ah! That's a different matter. You'd need the help of a manuscript archaeologist. That's someone who studies old papers. Using special scientific instruments, they would analyse the binding and paper fibres, the ink . . .'

As Dad went on, Evie stared at the ceiling, wondering what he was talking about.

Fortunately, Mum arrived home just then,

rescuing them from Dad's long explanation. Coming into the kitchen, she spotted the empty bean cans on the worktop and said, 'Wow! Dad's special. Is there any left for me?'

She was tucking in a minute later. 'Mmm! Delicious!' she said. Dad looked proud, but even Josh noticed Mum's grin.

'What were you talking about when I came in?' she asked.

'I was just explaining,' said Dad, 'how to work out the age of an old book.'

'Well, that's easy enough,' said Mum. 'Just take it to a bookshop that deals in rare books. There's one in town, Wick's I think it's called. I bet they'd know.'

'Where is it, Mum?' said Evie eagerly.

'Why do you want to know?' asked Josh inquisitively.

'It's for my history project,' Evie said quickly.

That night, Evie pulled the diary from under her pillow, picked up her rose-scented gel pen and began to write.

Dear diary,

I had an amazing morning with Beth at ballet. We're doing a school project about The Malkova

Dance Academy, and Miss Connie told us all about it! Then —

Suddenly, Evie's cheeks burned and she couldn't write another word. She had a plan, but couldn't tell it to anyone — not even her diary! It was like keeping a secret from her best friend and she squirmed inside.

Evie felt so desperate to understand her diary that she had decided to ask the experts about it. After school on Monday, on the way home from Jessica's, she was going to the bookshop!

She closed the diary, slipped it back under her pillow and tried to sleep.

Chapter Five

Ask No Questions

On Monday morning, Evie woke feeling worried. She hadn't checked her diary on Sunday, and now she was still putting it off. First, she put on her school uniform. Then she went downstairs and ate her porridge. Then she carefully packed her bag. Finally, having run out of excuses, she went back to her room and put her hand under her pillow.

She noticed the familiar soft tingle as her fingers touched the cover, but it seemed weaker than usual. Anxiously, she turned the pages, then trembled with relief when she saw the beautiful curly writing of the diary's reply.

Dear Evie,

Your project about the dance academy sounds most interesting. I'm sure you'll enjoy finding out all about it.

Discovery and understanding are wonderful, and there is much to learn through science. Remember, though, that not everything can be explained in this way.

Take your dancing, for example. There is a grace in the sweep of your arms and a harmony in your poise that is the magic of *your performance. But if you analyse it, the charm is lost.*

Some things, Evie, are best enjoyed and appreciated just as they are.

From your diary with love.

Evie snapped the diary shut and pushed it quickly into her bag. She understood the real message – it was saying don't ask too many questions about the diary!

Why won't it just explain how it works? Evie thought grumpily. It was *so* frustrating! Hadn't she shown that she could keep a secret? She was determined to visit the bookshop after school.

The bell for the last lesson had hardly stopped ringing before the whole crew – Evie, Beth, Lauren, Meera and Jess – was at the school gate.

Joking and laughing, they walked slowly towards Jess's house, planning to work together on their history projects.

'Mum said we could have chocolate muffins and milkshakes,' said Jess as they turned into her road.

'Yummy!' said Lauren and Meera at exactly the same time, and started giggling.

'Here we are,' said Jess, stopping beside a huge metal gate. It hung between two pillars, each topped with a large stone lion. Behind it, a long driveway led to an enormous old house covered with twisting vines stretching towards its roof.

'Wow!' said Evie. 'It's almost like a castle!'

'Probably to protect us from St Hilda's!' laughed Beth.

'What?' said Evie. 'Lottie's school?'

'Yes,' said Meera. 'It's only round the corner. It's really posh.'

'Oh, dear!' said Evie. 'Are all the girls as scary as Lottie?'

'No,' chuckled Lauren. 'Some of them are even worse!'

Evie tried to laugh, but just talking about Lottie made her feel anxious. She looked nervously over her shoulder and her mouth fell open. On the other pavement, dressed in their grey St Hilda's blazers, were Olivia, Grace and Lottie! All three crossed over the road.

'What are you doing here, Denham?' sneered Olivia.

'Yeah!' added Lottie. 'This road looked quite tidy till you came along.'

'Oi!' said Beth, flushing with anger. 'Just because Evie has more talent in her little toe than you have in your whole body, it doesn't mean you need to be spiteful!'

'Oh, amazing!' said Grace, poking Beth's arm

with her finger. 'A talking monkey? Perhaps we should take it home as a pet!'

Lottie laughed and was about to make another comment when she spotted the Malkova project folder sticking out of Beth's rucksack. Since spying on Evie and Beth in the principal's office, Lottie had been dying to know what they were up to. She couldn't ask, of course, so she turned to Jess, hoping for a clue.

Waving her arm at Beth and Evie, she asked, 'What are you doing bringing these ... strays home with you? Playing dollies?'

'If you must know –' Jess began.

'Don't waste your breath,' said Beth. 'They're not worth it!'

'You're right!' said Jess. 'Come on, girls. Let's go!'

Together they turned away and walked through the gate. As Evie pushed it shut, she could hear Grace talking.

'They are *so* annoying! Especially Beth and Evie.'

'You're telling me!' said Lottie crossly, then whispered, 'Listen. You remember I said they were talking to Miss Connie after ballet on Saturday?'

'Yes,' said Grace and Olivia, leaning forwards.

From behind the gate Evie leaned forwards too, trying to catch what Lottie was saying.

'Well,' Lottie continued, 'I want to know what they're doing. The trouble is, I have to go to my grandparents' wedding anniversary party on Wednesday . . . yawn! . . . which means I'll miss dance class. But you're going, aren't you?'

Olivia and Grace nodded.

'Good,' said Lottie. 'Then stay near them, OK? We've got to find out what's going on!'

Wishing Lottie had not been whispering, Evie turned away and followed the others up the driveway.

Chapter Six

A Lost Friend

The whole crew lay on the grass at the end of Jess's garden, discussing their projects.

Beth had said twice about finding Dame Malkova's marriage certificate in the parish records, but each time Evie's thoughts wandered.

She felt like a secret agent: unable to mention her diary, she couldn't explain that she had to leave early to go to the bookshop.

Just then, Jess's mum crossed the lawn carrying a tray piled high with home-made chocolate muffins.

'There's plenty more in the kitchen,' she said, laying the tray on the ground. 'And strawberry milkshakes are on the way!'

'Wow! Thanks, Mrs Whittington!' they all said, diving for the plate.

All except Evie. Knowing the bookshop would shut soon, she felt so nervous she couldn't eat a thing.

'I'm really sorry, Jess,' she said, 'but I don't feel very hungry. Mum said I mustn't be late home, so I'd better go.'

'Oh, stay!' everyone said together.

'My mum would drive you home,' said Jess.

'I don't want to be any trouble,' said Evie, quickly shoving her pencil case into her bag. 'See you tomorrow.'

Then she hurried down the driveway, hoping to escape before Mrs Whittington offered her a lift.

Ten minutes later, Evie stood in the high street looking up at the flaking gold paint that read 'Wick's Bookshop'. Cupping her hands to the glass of the higgledy-piggledy windowpanes, Evie stared inside.

It looked dusty and forgotten, just shelves and boxes crammed with hundreds of yellowing books. With her heart pounding, Evie pushed open the door.

A bell above the door swung, its clang echoing through the shop. Evie turned to run away. *This is a silly idea!* she thought. *I should never have come.*

Then, before she could escape, a voice called out, 'Hello, my dear. What can I do for you?'

Evie jumped as a man with wispy grey hair and a woolly cardigan popped up from a hatch in the floor.

'Sorry if I shocked you,' he said, smiling kindly. 'I was just fetching some old paperbacks from the cellar.' Evie breathed a sigh of relief.

'I'm Mr Wick,' he continued, clambering from the hatch. He carefully dropped a box full of books on an old table in the middle of the shop. A great cloud of dust billowed up and he flapped his arms, trying to waft it away.

Before Evie could speak, Mr Wick spotted her diary poking from her bag and his face lit up.

'Have you come to ask about that?' he said.

'Mm-mm,' stuttered Evie, lifting it out and placing it carefully on the table. 'I'm, um, doing a history project and wondered –'

'If I could tell you about it?' he said. 'Of course. Let's have a look.'

He switched on a bright lamp and inspected the diary so closely it looked as though he was smelling it!

'Well,' he said, raising his eyebrows. 'Most interesting. See this binding here? That makes it at least a hundred years old. It may even be a diary. I wonder if anyone has written in it?'

Evie gasped, wanting to grab her diary and run out of the shop. Why hadn't she thought? It was obvious that he would want to look inside! He'd see every word she had written!

'Er, thank you for your help,' said Evie, reaching out her hand. 'May I take it home now, please?'

'Oh, no, Miss. We've hardly begun! The next thing is to take a look inside.'

Evie began to tremble as Mr Wick selected a pair of tweezers from his drawer and carefully turned the first page.

She held her breath till her eyes bulged, then

suddenly let it out in a puff of relief that blew a
fresh cloud of dust all over Mr Wick. The pages
were blank! All her entries had disappeared!

Then, in a panic, she remembered the rhyme
on the first page.

. . . if anyone finds out,
These words will fade,
and I'll be gone . . .

Terrified that by not listening to her diary's advice she had lost her wonderful friend forever, Evie gabbled, 'Oh, please, please can I take it now?'

'You youngsters,' said Mr Wick, shaking his head slowly. 'So impatient.'

'But –'

'This is fascinating,' continued Mr Wick calmly, and reached into his drawer for a padded envelope. 'But to reveal the truth we need to send it away to a laboratory.'

Evie looked so horrified he patted her hand. 'Don't you worry, dear. It'll only take a couple of days. Now, while I write the address, perhaps you can tell me where you got it from?'

With tears filling her eyes, Evie spluttered, 'Sorry, I'm late for dinner,' and ran from the shop without her diary, leaving the doorbell clanging in the dusty silence.

Chapter Seven

The Spying Game

That night, Evie couldn't sleep. Her bed sheet peeled off the mattress and tangled itself round her legs as she twisted and turned. Every time her eyes shut, she saw a blank diary page and, certain that she'd broken the magic spell, she cried herself to sleep.

The next morning, tired and anxious, hoping it had been a terrible dream, she searched all round her bed . . . but her dear, dear diary was not there.

At school that day, and the next, Mr Mitchin's voice seemed to come from a faraway room. Every tick-tock of the clock seemed to last an hour.

On Wednesday evening, Dad dropped her off at the academy for jazz dance. She'd been so slow getting ready that by the time she was changed the warm-up had finished.

'OK, class,' Miss Connie called out. 'Now we're all here, I'd like to continue where we left off last week. The *chassé* is tricky, but if you concentrate, I'm sure you'll manage. Evie, please go first.'

Evie hadn't warmed up and started on the

wrong foot. She tried to correct herself and bumped into Beth.

'Never mind, Evie. You can try again in a minute. Olivia, perhaps you could lead today?'

'Whatever's the matter?' Beth whispered when Evie joined her. 'You've been like a zombie for the last two days.'

'Nothing,' Evie mumbled, staring at the floor.

'Well, there obviously *is* something,' said Beth matter-of-factly. 'If you don't want to talk about it, that's fine, and if you do, that's fine too. But, whichever it is, just cheer up!'

Beth was right, of course. Evie gave a weak smile and stood up straight. Dance class was the highlight of the week, so why waste it by moping around!

Olivia finished her turn. Then, instead of standing with Grace at the other end of the room, she smiled and stood right next to Evie!

Beth caught Evie's eye and pulled a what's-this-all-about face. Evie shrugged.

Later, as they performed a routine in pairs, Evie whispered to Beth. 'Maybe she's sorry for being horrible when we went to Jess's?'

'Yeah,' said Beth with a grin. 'And maybe Mr Mitchin will become a prima ballerina!'

A picture of Mr Mitchin in a tutu skipped through Evie's imagination and she nearly burst out laughing. Giggling and stumbling, she held on to Beth's arm, at which Miss Connie clapped loudly.

'Thank you, class,' she said with a loud sigh. 'I think we'll stop there. It's the big football match tonight and I know some of you want to get home early.'

Evie saw Mrs Swann nodding enthusiastically.

'And do *please* try to remember the routine by next week,' added Miss Connie.

Everyone mumbled, 'Yes, Miss Connie,' and trotted to the changing rooms.

Mrs Swann put away the music books and, slipping a green and white shawl around her shoulders, scuttled towards the door. As she passed Evie and Beth, she whispered, 'Miss Connie said you two were doing a project on the academy.'

'Yes,' the girls nodded.

'I thought it was a lovely idea,' said Mrs Swann. 'So I looked out some photos for you. I'm off to the football now, but I've left them on my desk. Do pop up and get them before you leave.'

'Oh! Thank you!' they gasped.

As Evie and Beth changed, Olivia stood behind the next row of lockers, listening in on their chat.

'It's weird, Mrs Swann going to the match,' said Evie. 'I never think of little old ladies watching football.'

'My granny's a little old lady,' said Beth, 'and she loves it. She even shouts at the TV if her side is losing!'

'I don't think I'll ever like football,' said Evie. 'Not when I could watch ballet instead.'

'Hurry up, slowcoach,' said Beth, holding the door open. 'I'll race you up to Mrs Swann's office. Let's see what's there.'

A low gasp came from behind the lockers.

Evie had just picked up her bag. 'What's that?' she said.

'I didn't hear anything,' said Beth. 'Come on, let's go.'

As they climbed the stairs to Mrs Swann's office, Olivia crept from the changing room and padded after them.

Evie and Beth were searching through the
papers on the desk looking for the photos when
the door creaked and began to open.

'Who's there?' said Evie. The door stopped
moving, but no one answered, so they carried on
searching.

'I've found it,' said Beth, holding up a thick
yellow folder.

'Well done!' said Evie. 'Now we'd better tidy up.
We don't want to leave a mess.'

They quickly straightened all the papers and
hurried through the door with Evie clutching the
folder. Olivia pressed herself against the wall,
clapping her hand over her mouth in case she
squealed, but the movement caught Beth's eye.

'Olivia? What are you doing here?'

'Oh! I was ... um ... looking for Mrs Swann.'

'OK, see you then,' said Beth. Then, as they
walked down the stairs, she whispered to Evie,

'Did you see how guilty she looked? She was *so* up to something!'

Chapter Eight

Past Tense

Mum was lucky. She was working late at the hospital where it was quiet.

Evie, however, lay on her bed with her hands pressed tightly over her ears, trying to blot out the terrible din from the sitting room.

'Yeeesss!' roared Dad. 'Gooooaaaal!'

'No waaay! Come off it, ref!' screamed Charlie.

'Penalty!' yelled Josh.

Evie wished the tickets hadn't sold out so quickly, because it meant Dad, Charlie and Josh were shouting at the TV instead of doing it at the football ground.

Since dance class, all Evie wanted was some peace. She had tried reading a comic, drawing and even tidying her wardrobe! Nothing helped; she couldn't stop thinking about her diary.

Her tummy churned with a dreadful sadness. It was the same sick feeling she'd had when they moved house and left her best friend Hannah behind. Now she'd left her diary behind and it was all her fault.

Suddenly, a wail like three police sirens came from downstairs. 'Noo-oo! Noo-oo! Noooooooo!' cried three voices, then silence ... Millchester had lost the match! They were out of the Cup!

Evie felt a little sorry for them, but losing a football game was nothing like as bad as losing your best friend.

With the football over it was quiet again, and Evie turned off her light. In the darkness, dreams of empty pages filled her head again, and once more the bed sheet wound itself around her fidgety legs. *I'm never going to get to sleep*, Evie thought, and then she had an idea. She sat up in bed and turned on her light.

After rummaging quietly in her schoolbag she pulled out a notebook and pen, turned to a clean page, and began to write:

Dear diary,
  I wish I hadn't —

Evie squirmed. She couldn't think what to say and ripped out the page, scrumpled it into a tight ball and threw it in her bin. Taking a deep breath, she tried again:

Dear diary,

I feel so sad. I don't know what —

'Oh,' she groaned under her breath. 'This doesn't feel right.' She snatched out the page, tore it into tiny pieces and dropped them into the bin. They tumbled like snowflakes, reminding Evie of a Russian winter from a film she had seen. Then

she thought of Dame Malkova: how hard it must have been for her as a young girl all those years ago.

Suddenly she remembered the photos, and reached for the folder on her bedside table. She lay it on her lap and lifted out a thick bundle held together by an elastic band.

The pictures were black and white, or tea-stain brown, and many were curled up or creased, but Evie shook her head slowly, stunned to recognise the studio from all those years ago – it looked just the same as it did now!

Staring at the grainy, faded pictures, Evie saw girls in full tulle skirts stretching at the *barre* and performing *arabesques*. Apart from their clothes, nothing had changed in a hundred years!

She picked up a photo of a beautiful lady in a flowing gown observing a young dancer. Evie held it near the lamp, thinking back to the painting from *Coppélia* in Mrs Swann's office. *Perhaps this is Dame Malkova!* she thought.

The lady wore a beaded scarf over her head. Her eyes seemed to shine with the joy of the girl's dance, and Evie felt that the photographer had captured a perfect, magical moment in time.

Maybe the quiet beauty of the ballet was what Dame Malkova really wanted, thought Evie. *Maybe the only*

way she could truly enjoy the dance was to escape from
the excitement of fame.

Evie sighed. *This is proper history*, she thought.
*Not just dates and places, but real lives of real people . . .
and that's exactly what the diary was trying to tell me!*

*Finding out facts won't explain its magic, and now
I've spoiled it! Oh, why didn't I listen? Well, I can't
wait until after school – I'll have to go to the bookshop
first thing tomorrow!*

Evie popped the photos back in the folder and
curled up under her duvet. As she drifted off to
sleep a wonderful idea floated into her mind –
Dame Malkova's wish would make a perfect end
to the project!

Chapter Nine

The Reunion

Brown milk dribbled down Josh's chin as he spooned the last Choccy Crispies from his cereal bowl. Mum sipped a cup of tea and stared sleepily out the window.

'*Please* can we go now, Mum?' said Evie, jigging by the kitchen door with her hair neatly brushed, her bag packed and her coat buttoned to her chin.

'There's plenty of time, love. I'll just finish my tea, then we'll leave.'

'It's just . . .'

Evie hesitated. She couldn't tell Mum why she was in such a hurry . . .

They set off, but had only reached Mrs Volkov's gate when Josh realised he'd left his PE kit behind. Evie grumbled to herself, worrying that Mr Wick might have lost the diary; after all, his shop was in a terrible muddle. Or, even worse, what if he had discovered the mysterious writing and wouldn't let her have it back?

Eventually they reached the bookshop and Evie said, 'Mum, could I pop in here for a minute? I need to collect something for a project.'

'Can't it wait till after school?'

'I'd *really* like to get it now. Please.'

'OK then. In we go.'

'Er, it's only a small shop,' said Evie, wanting to avoid difficult explanations about the diary. 'Why don't you and Josh wait out here?'

'No,' said Mum. 'It's best if we all stay together.'

Hoping to get to the counter quickly, Evie shoved open the door and rushed in – and collided with a little old lady who was coming out!

'I'm *so* sorry!' stammered Evie.

'Never mind, dear,' said the lady, looking up.

'Oh!' exclaimed Evie. It was Mrs Volkov!

'You hurry in,' she whispered, 'while I have a word with your mum.'

Mr Wick recognised Evie at once.

'Here it is,' he said, holding up the diary.

Evie's head swam. Her cheeks flushed. 'Thank

you!' she whispered happily and leaned forwards
to take it.

'Hold on!' said Mr Wick, snatching it back.
'Don't you want to know what I found out?'

'Yes, please,' said Evie. 'But I must hurry.'

'I know it's here somewhere,' he said, slowly
turning each page.

'Please, I must go, or I'll be late for school,'
said Evie frantically.

'Ah, this is it!' he said, as if he hadn't heard.
'Do you see this watermark?'

Evie nodded, though she couldn't see a thing.

'The laboratory said it was the mark of a local
printer. Sadly, it's nothing special. Just a pretty
Victorian sketchbook.' He pushed the book across
the counter.

'Oh, thank you!' said Evie, grabbing the diary
and hugging it tightly. She knew it *was* special!

I'm so thrilled to have you back, she thought.

I've really missed you!

'I'd still like to hear where you found it,' said Mr Wick, but already the doorbell was clanging and Evie was back outside, with her diary tucked safely in her bag.

Smiling gently at Evie, Mrs Volkov raised her eyebrows and gave a delicate nod. 'Well, I'd better let you go,' she said, and tottered off, her walking stick clacking on the pavement.

At school, it was break time before Evie could be alone. As the others ran to the playground she hid in the toilets, locked the door and lovingly drew the diary from her bag. Goose pimples prickled her neck as the strongest tingle she'd ever felt tickled her fingers. She eased open the cover.

'Oh!' she exclaimed, thrilled to see writing.

Dear Evie,

I'm so pleased you came to collect me, and I look forward to hearing your news.

I hope you learned what you wanted from Mr Wick. Making your own decisions is important, but it's also good to consider the advice others give you.

Evie gulped, realising how close she had come to losing her diary forever. She slipped it gently back into her bag and skipped to the playground to find Beth.

It didn't matter that she hadn't found out how her diary sent its wonderful messages – some things, she understood, are best enjoyed just the way they are.

Small groups of sad-faced pupils huddled in little groups, so when Evie bounced up with a beaming smile Beth spotted her straight away.

'You're the only one not moping about yesterday's football,' she said. 'What's made you so happy?'

'Er . . .' said Evie, thinking quickly so she didn't mention the real reason. 'Because I've had a great idea about our project!'

'Let's get away from all these miseries,' said Beth, 'then you can tell me about it!' They linked arms and wandered to a quiet corner near the school kitchen.

'You know the last thing Miss Connie said about Dame Malkova?'

'What?' said Beth. 'That she wanted to pass on her love of dance as a gift to others?'

'Exactly!' said Evie. 'Well, why don't we put in photos of all the current pupils at the academy. It'll show that her love of dance really has been passed on to others!'

'That's a fantastic idea!' said Beth. 'I'll ask my mum to bring her camera to class on Saturday!'

Chapter Ten

The Misunderstanding

The following Wednesday, Evie arrived early for jazz class. She carried Mrs Swann's photograph folder in a supermarket bag, hoping to return it before the lesson started.

She climbed the creaky stairs towards the principal's office, paused in front of the big wooden door, took a deep breath and knocked.

'Come in.'

Evie stepped inside and stopped with a jolt. Behind the desk sat Mrs Swann, frowning darkly. Beside her stood Miss Connie . . . and by the fireplace were Lottie and Olivia, grinning smugly!

Feeling scared and confused, Evie swallowed hard.

'Please sit down,' said Mrs Swann, pointing to two empty chairs placed in front of her desk. Evie sat on one without saying a word.

'Earlier today,' said Mrs Swann, 'Lottie and Olivia came to see me about a most serious issue. It concerns both you and Bethany Dickinson. I had hoped she'd be here by now, but we must get on without her as it's nearly time for class.'

Evie felt muddled, wondering what it was all about and wishing that Beth were with her.

'Now, Evie. I'm going to ask Lottie and Olivia to tell you exactly what they told me. I will then ask you to explain yourself, but please think very carefully before you answer. OK, Lottie. Please begin.'

'She,' said Lottie, pointing at Evie, 'is a thief!'

'What?' Evie gasped.

'Yeah!' continued Lottie. 'We've found you out, Denham!'

'You can't deny it. I saw you last week, stealing from this office!' added Olivia.

Evie tried to speak but no words came out. Her ears burned and her hands shook so badly that she dropped her carrier bag, spilling the yellow folder on to the floor.

'That's it!' Olivia squealed, pointing at the folder. 'That's what she stole! We've caught her red-handed.'

'Didn't I say so!' said Lottie loudly, turning to Mrs Swann. 'That's proof! You've *got* to call her parents and expel her from the academy! Maybe you should call the police too: they'd come if we had a thief at St Hilda's.'

How can they say these things? Evie thought, as tears rolled down her cheeks.

'Thank you, Lottie. Thank you, Olivia, I think I've heard enough,' said Mrs Swann. Then she leaned forwards and gave Evie a tissue.

As Evie dried her eyes, Mrs Swann seemed to smile sadly.

'When you feel ready, Evie,' she said gently, 'would you show us what's in that folder?'

Still trembling, Evie stood up and laid the folder on the desk, revealing the photographs.

'Lottie. Olivia. What do you see?' asked Mrs Swann sternly.

'Er, some old photos,' mumbled Lottie.

'Exactly! Photos that I lent to Evie and Bethany for use in their class project.'

'But I saw them taking stuff off your desk!' said Olivia.

'Yes, because I asked them to come up here and collect it!'

Both Lottie and Olivia blushed hotly.

'Please don't look at the floor when I'm speaking to you, Lottie,' said Mrs Swann. 'I hope you now realise that you should never make an accusation unless you are *very* certain of your facts.'

An urgent knock on the door spared Lottie further embarrassment.

'Come in,' called Mrs Swann.

The door flew open and Beth rushed in with a huge grin on her face.

'Sorry I'm late,' she said breathlessly. 'I had to stay behind at school.'

'It doesn't —' began Mrs Swann.

'Guess what?' Beth said. 'We've got our project back!'

'That's —' began Mrs Swann again, then

chuckled as Beth carried on.

'Mr Mitchin said he was really impressed by the way we showed Dame Malkova's love of dance, and gave us top marks!'

Mrs Swann clapped her hands and laughed. 'How wonderful!'

'Well done, girls!' said Miss Connie, and smiled fondly at Evie.

Lottie and Olivia, who looked as miserable as wet kittens, had not said a word since Beth arrived.

'Come on, you two,' said Mrs Swann cheerfully. 'Congratulate them on their success.'

'Oh, well *done*,' said Lottie, through clenched teeth.

'Mm, yeah, great,' muttered Olivia.

Mrs Swann raised her eyebrows. 'Well, now that's cleared up, you'd better hurry to the studio. We don't want to keep the others waiting.'

Chatting excitedly, Evie and Beth clattered downstairs to the changing room and slipped on their jazz shoes.

'Go on in, Beth,' said Evie, who was deliberately fumbling with her laces. 'I won't be long.'

When Beth had closed the door, Evie picked up her bag and patted it.

'I'm so sorry,' she said gently to the diary nestled inside. 'Sorry for trying to test your magic.'

'Evie,' called Miss Connie from the corridor. 'Are you ready?'

'Just coming!' said Evie, and quickly hung her bag on a peg. She turned to go, then paused . . . 'Thank you, diary,' she whispered. 'Thank you for being such a loyal friend.'

Dancing Diva

Show everyone you're a ballet star with all the info on the coolest ballet positions!

Glissade

A sliding step, which you can do in any direction and is normally used as a joining step.

Arabesque

Your body is supported on one leg while the other leg is extended behind at 90 degrees. Your arms are also extended to give you the longest line possible from your fingertips to your toes.

Find more cool ballet moves in the next From Your Diary With Love book

Jeté

A jump from one leg to another where the working leg looks like it's thrown forwards, backwards or sideways.

What's Your Sleepover Style?

Work your way through the quiz to see what you love most about sleepovers!

1. On a Saturday you're normally . . .

a. At the cinema watching the latest movie
b. Practising your dance moves for the next disco
c. Hitting the shops to try a new look

2. You dream of being just like . . .

a. Hilary Duff
b. Girls Aloud
c. Ashley Tisdale

3. When you and your mates hang out you . . .

a. Pretend you're film stars
b. Make out you're a girl band
c. Give each other cool new hairstyles

4. At school, your fave thing is...

a. Being in school plays
b. Music lessons, where you can show off your talents
c. Lunchtime, when you have a gossip over the latest mags

5.

Get busy making this cool top to help you to remember your sleepover forever!

Sleepover Souvenir

What you need:

Plain T-shirt
Fabric pens
Glitter-glue pen
Your friends

What to do:

1. Check with your parents that they're happy for you to customise your top!

2. Think about what you'd like to have on your T-shirt and what would make you remember your sleepover most. Maybe your friends autographs or what you've been up to together

3. Next, make your own designs on the T-shirt and adding your own cool words and pictures. Use fabric pens and glitter glue pens for customising cool!

4. You can either wear the T-shirt or hang it up like a poster to remind you of all the cool times you've had

Darcey Bussell

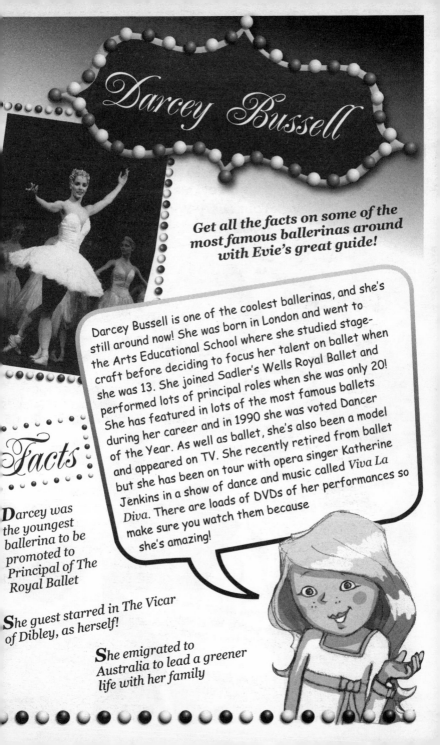

Get all the facts on some of the most famous ballerinas around with Evie's great guide!

Darcey Bussell is one of the coolest ballerinas, and she's still around now! She was born in London and went to the Arts Educational School where she studied stage-craft before deciding to focus her talent on ballet when she was 13. She joined Sadler's Wells Royal Ballet and performed lots of principal roles when she was only 20! She has featured in lots of the most famous ballets during her career and in 1990 she was voted Dancer of the Year. As well as ballet, she's also been a model and appeared on TV. She recently retired from ballet but she has been on tour with opera singer Katherine Jenkins in a show of dance and music called *Viva La Diva*. There are loads of DVDs of her performances so make sure you watch them because she's amazing!

Facts

Darcey was the youngest ballerina to be promoted to Principal of The Royal Ballet

She guest starred in *The Vicar of Dibley*, as herself!

She emigrated to Australia to lead a greener life with her family

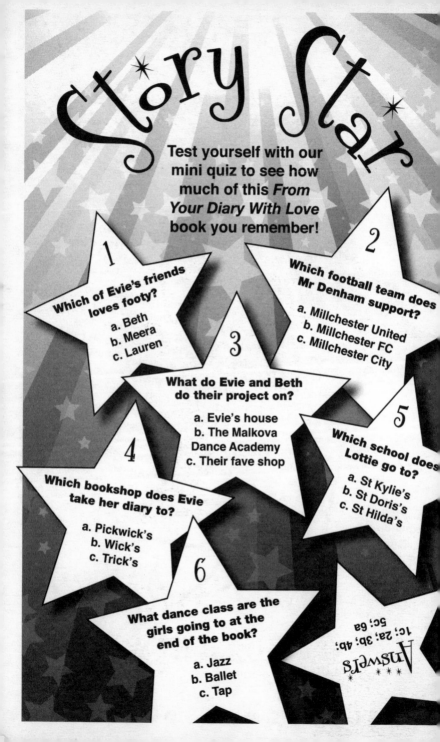

Can't wait for the next book in the series? Here's a sneak preview of

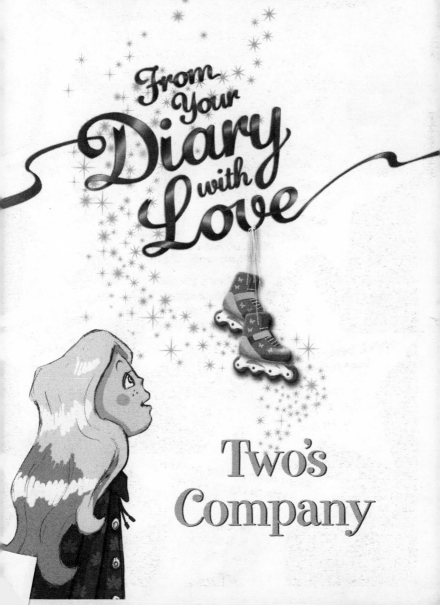

From Your Diary with Love

Two's Company

Chapter One

Three's a Crowd

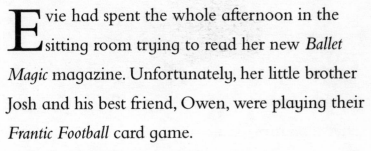

Evie had spent the whole afternoon in the sitting room trying to read her new *Ballet Magic* magazine. Unfortunately, her little brother Josh and his best friend, Owen, were playing their *Frantic Football* card game.

'Goal!' yelled Josh gleefully, throwing down his last card.

'Disallowed!' screamed Owen, slapping a

referee card on top.

'That's not fair! I was out!'

'But you started first, so I've got one more go!'

Mum came in just as Evie, with a cushion pressed over each ear, wailed 'Pleeease shut up!'

'Come on, Evie, love,' Mum said, and led her to the quiet of the kitchen. 'How do you fancy inviting Beth round? She can join us for tea then you could watch a film or something.'

'Thanks, Mum,' said Evie. 'That would be brilliant! I *so* need a break from those two!'

Beth arrived as Dad was phoning out for a gigantic teatime pizza, and soon Evie's miserable afternoon turned into a real treat.

They were sitting on the stairs trying to decide what to do, when the pizza-delivery bike stopped outside. Beth grinned and gave Evie a nudge.

'Let's play a trick!' she said, and ran to the front door. Just as the boy was about to knock they yanked it open and screamed. The poor boy was so shocked he almost dropped the pizza, and they ran away giggling while Dad apologised and paid the bill.

'Mmm, this is good!' said Mum as they sat round the table.

'Well, I'm a very talented cook,' said Dad.

'Ha, ha,' said Evie, then whispered to Beth, 'Sorry, he always says that!'

'Oh, I nearly forgot,' said Dad. 'I'm bagging the TV this evening. There's an interesting programme about pensions I'd like to see. You can watch it too, if you like.'

'That's *really* kind of you,' said Evie, 'but I think we'll go to my room.'

For a while, they sat on Evie's bed playing CDs and chatting about their morning ballet lesson at The Malkova Dance Academy.

Then Beth's favourite song came on. She jumped up, grabbed Evie's hairbrush for a microphone, and began to sing along. Evie joined in immediately, cupping her hands over her ears like studio headphones and swaying to the tune.

'Hey!' said Beth when the CD finished. 'Why don't we make up our own dance?'

'Yes!' said Evie excitedly. 'We'll need more room, though.'

'Could we push your bed against the wall?'

'Good idea!' said Evie. 'You take that end.'

They shoved it across the floor, but Evie's hand caught her pillow, revealing the purple cover of an old book. Quickly, she covered it up, hoping

Beth hadn't spotted it – she couldn't let anyone, not even her closest friend in Crossacre, discover the secret of that book. It was her special diary.

° * ° ° ° ° * * * ° ° * * ° ° **

With the floor clear, Evie pressed 'play' and Beth began to dance. As she tried all sorts of slides and turns, Evie scribbled everything down on a notepad. Then they swapped round, with Beth calling out the steps as Evie matched the routine exactly to the music.

At the end of the song Evie felt puffed out, so they swapped again.

'For this routine,' said Evie in a posh announcer's voice, 'you must dance in the style of Miss Lottie Dean.'

Beth leaped up, smiling like a beauty queen, and bowed. Then she flounced, strutted and waved her arms around with such exaggerated flourishes that Evie fell off the bed laughing!

Suddenly, there came a knock and the door flew open. There stood Josh wearing Dad's hat and coat, and Owen with a felt-tip pen moustache, carrying Mum's umbrella. They marched into the room and sat on Evie's bed.

'We are the judges!' said Josh.

'And we think your dance is pants!' Owen added.

'So you are sentenced to a million years in prison!' said Josh.

'GET OUT!' shouted Evie, shoving them on to the landing and slamming the door behind them, then propping a chair against the door. 'Shall we start again from the top?'

They turned the volume up full and began slowly. Then something clicked: each step synchronised perfectly, their timing was spot-on, every move rolled seamlessly to the next.

'Yayyyy! That was brilliant!' gasped Beth.

'Let's –' said Evie, but stopped dead with her mouth open. Dad's head was poking round the door and he *must* have seen them dancing!

'I knocked,' he shouted, holding out the phone, 'but you didn't hear. Anyway, it's Hannah for you.'

Instantly forgetting her embarrassment, Evie grabbed the handset.

'Hannah! How are you?'

Beth paused the CD and sat on the bed, kicking her legs.

'I know! I can't believe it!' Evie squealed into the phone. 'All day together in London! It'll be fantastic!'

After ten minutes of wondering if the call could possibly last any longer, Beth stood up. Obviously,

it could! She pressed 'stop' on the CD player and stared out the window.

'And when we've finished the shops,' Evie continued, 'Mum said we might go to a show! Which one do you fancy?'

Beth crossed her arms and frowned . . . but Evie, smiling happily, was so excited she didn't notice.

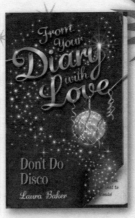